Just in Time for New Year's!

A Harry & Emily Adventure

Karen Gray Ruelle

Holiday House / New York

In memory of my Nana Sallie,
the best snorer in Brooklyn

Reading level: 2.6

Text and illustrations copyright © 2004 by Karen Gray Ruelle
All Rights Reserved
Printed in the United States of America
www.holidayhouse.com
First Edition
1 3 5 7 9 10 8 6 4 2

Library of Congress Cataloging-in-Publication Data
Ruelle, Karen Gray.
Just in time for New Year's!: a Harry and Emily adventure / Karen Gray Ruelle.—
1st ed.
p. cm.
Summary: Cat siblings Harry and Emily try to stay up
until midnight on New Year's Eve.
ISBN 0-8234-1841-3 (hardcover)
ISBN 0-8234-1842-1 (paperback)
[1. New Year—Fiction. 2. Brothers and sisters—Fiction.
3. Cats—Fiction.] I. Title.
PZ7.R88525Hap 2004
[E]—dc22
2003064728

contents

1.
ZZZZZZZZZ

Every night, Emily heard snoring.

Every morning,

she told her brother, Harry.

"I do not snore," said Harry.

"Yes, you do," said Emily.

"You should make a New Year's

resolution to stop snoring."

"I do not snore!" said Harry.

"When is New Year's Eve anyway?"
    asked Emily.
"New Year's Eve is in four days,"
    said their mother.
"Can we stay up
    until midnight this year?" asked Harry.
    Their mother and father
    looked at each other.

Their father said, "I think you are both old enough now. If you can s awake until midnight,
we will all celebrate together."
"Hooray!" said Harry and Emily.
"We have three nights to practice," said Harry.
"What will we practice?" asked Emily.
"We will practice staying up late," said Harry.
"Your snoring will keep us both awake," said Emily.
"How do you know I snore if you are asleep?" asked Harry.
"Your snores are very loud. I can hear them in my sleep," said Emily.

2. Practice

"Emily! Harry!
    Please set the table,"
    said their mother.
"We can't!" said Emily.
"We are too busy practicing."
"What are you practicing?"
    asked their mother.
"We are practicing staying awake
    for New Year's Eve," said Harry.
"I see," said their mother.
"Please set the table.
    You can practice later."

After dinner Harry and Emily
thought of ways to stay awake.
They thought of taking daytime naps.
They thought of holding
their eyelids open.
They thought of opening the windows
to let in the cold air.

They practiced staying up late.

That night, they stayed up until 9:30.

"We have to practice harder,"
said Harry.

"Or else we will never stay up
until midnight."

The next night, they practiced harder.

They fell asleep at 8:30.

"This is not working," said Harry.

On the third day, they took a nap.

It was not a long nap.

That night they stayed awake
until 8:00.
"We will have to take more naps
or we will not be able to stay awake
until midnight," said Harry.
"Don't worry," said Emily.
"I'm sure your snores will wake us up."

3.
Noisemakers
and Party Hats

On the big day,

Harry and Emily took two naps.

But they could not sleep.

They were much too excited.

Instead, they talked about

New Year's Eve.

What would it be like

to stay up until midnight?

It would be so dark out!
Would the stars look different
at midnight?
Would the moon be out?

After dinner Harry and Emily's
mother said,
"Let's get ready for New Year's Eve."
They got noisemakers.
They got bubbly drinks
made out of juice and seltzer.
They got party hats.

"Let's practice the countdown,"
said their father.
"Ten, nine, eight, seven, six,
five, four, three, two . . .
HAPPY NEW YEAR!"
They blew their noisemakers.
They drank their bubbly drinks.
They shouted and they sang.
Then their mother said,
"That was great!"

"I can't wait until midnight!"
  said Emily.

"Go brush your teeth,"
  said their mother.

"Then you will be all ready."

"When will it be midnight?"
  asked Emily.

"It is only 9:00.
  You still have three hours,"
  said their father.

  Harry and Emily ran upstairs
  and brushed their teeth.
  They played a board game.

They listened to holiday music
to put them in a holiday mood.
"Is it midnight yet?" asked Emily.
"It is only 10:00," said Harry.
They opened the windows
to let in the cold air.
They played some more music.

"Now what time is it?" asked Emily.

"It is 10:15," said Harry.

"It will never be midnight," said Emily.

"What time is it now?" asked Emily.

"It is time to hold our eyelids open,"
  said Harry.

They sat on the floor
  and held open their eyelids.

The clock ticked.

"Time?" asked Emily.

There was no answer.

Harry was asleep.

Emily closed her eyes.

She would stay awake

with her eyes closed.

The clock ticked.

The house was very quiet.

Suddenly there was a loud snore.

Emily jumped up.

She looked at Harry.

But Harry was not snoring.

He was still fast asleep.

If Harry wasn't snoring,

then who was?

Emily closed her eyes again.

But that loud snoring

kept waking her up.

Then she had a great idea.

4.
countdown!

"Wake up!" said Emily.

"I have a great idea.

If snoring wakes us up,

so will other loud noises!"

She told Harry her idea.

He agreed that it might work.

They ran from room to room,
getting everything ready.
"It is 11:00," said Harry.
"We have one hour until midnight."

They spent some time

looking out the window.

There was no moon.

But there were so many stars!

"I think the stars

are brighter than ever," said Emily.

"I've never seen so many stars,"

said Harry.

They started counting stars.

They got as far as 76.

Then they fell fast asleep.

Emily woke up to a very loud snore.

She opened her eyes

and looked over at Harry.

But Harry was already awake.

He laughed and said,

"You were snoring!

You woke us both up

with your snores.

You are the one who snores, not me."

Emily was about
to say something.
Just then
they heard
a bell ringing.
Then another
bell started
to ring.
And another.
They heard
a chirping noise.
They heard loud music.
They heard loud beeps
and whistles.
All the alarm clocks
were going off!

"What is all that racket?"
 said their mother.
"What on earth is going on?"
 said their father.

Harry and Emily ran from room
to room,
turning off all the alarms.
Then they came into the living room
with party hats and noisemakers
and bubbly drinks.
"It's nearly midnight!" said Harry.
"Ten, nine, eight..."
"Seven, six, five...," Emily joined in.
Their parents joined in,

"Four, three, two..."

Then they all shouted together,
"HAPPY NEW YEAR!"